T0086282

HEARTFELT MOMENTS

KATHERINE OSTROM

authorHOUSE®

AuthorHouse™
1663 Liberty Drive
Bloomington, IN 47403
www.authorhouse.com
Phone: 1 (800) 839-8640

Published by AuthorHouse 11/19/2016

ISBN: 978-1-5246-4886-2 (sc)
ISBN: 978-1-5246-4885-5 (e)

Library of Congress Control Number: 2016919512

Print information available on the last page.

To Teddy O.

A HEALING TOUCH

Ring. Ring. I pick up the telephone.

"Hello."

A familiar voice greets me. "Kathy, how about attending a revival tonight? A friend of mine wants me to pick up around six thirty. I can get you along the wasy."

"Oh Mary. I broke my right middle finger over the weekend playing volleyball. It's in a cast."

She laughs stating, "You broke your finger! But you feel alright, don't you? Aw, come on gal, get out of the house. Ted won't mind. I'll pick you up around six o'clock." Click, and a dead dial tone.

Mary knew I face lonely hours while my husband works at a local fabricating plant until eleven o'clock p.m. I had no alternative but to reluctantly take a quick shower, and change into 'dressier' attire.

Mary honked her weather beaten van's horn around six fifteen. Climbing in the passenger's side I seated myself, double checking my safety belt buckle. Furiously, she drove ignoring all speed limit warning signs. Upon reaching a modest brick house I silently breathe a sign of relief. A beautiful dark tan woman warmly greets us. Assembling ourselves in Mary's vehicle we exchange names, and discuss directions to reach a neighboring Pentecostal church.

The service started at seven. We three scurry to front row seats. A handsome man introduces himself as a pastor. Nodding his head Shasta explains she invited us. He smiles, shaking our hands. Calmly he states, "I hope you enjoy the meeting."

I felt uneasiness as seats began filling up. Feeling very uncomfortable, I nudge Mary's ribs whispering, "Did you know this church is all black?"

"No, I did not. Shasta is half black though."

"Well," I answer, "The worst they can do is ask us to leave or run us out."

I sense every eyeball on us as the pastor spoke the opening statement. "We are pleased to have you come tonight for this special occasion. We welcome each and every one of you. You know with God Almighty all things are possible. He knows everything that happens in our lives. We don't know why these visitors came to this meeting. But God knows their circumstances and why they are here. The Lord knows no racial barriers. We welcomes all people in the body of Christ. He has no preferences. And this church is a God fearing and Holy Spirit filled church of God. Please make our visitors welcome. Give them a round of applause."

With enthusiasm, the choir delighted the audience singing in updated blues tempo. Clothed in beautiful navy satin robes they sway rhythmic to chords of popular religious hymns. Captured by divine sounds I thought, "Man, the angels in Heaven couldn't be better."

After listening to the guest speaker's message, I could not question God's Holy presence. Passionately he spoke of the Holy Spirit; why we must not doubt it; why we must trust and believe in it. If we believe in the Lord we had to believe in the Holy Spirit. Our lives could prosper; we could even be healed because that Spirit lives in us. When he closed the sermon, asking for the congregation to come forth for a blessing or healing, I did not hesitate.

Upon the stage I heard him ask, "Do you believe Jesus died on the cross for you sins?"

I reply, "I do."

"Do you believe in the Holy Spirit?"

"Yes."

"What do you wish for me to pray for you?"

I point to my cast. "I have a broken finger. It bugs me. I ask for healing."

He smiled, placing one hand on my forehead and another hand on my shoulder. He shouts, "In the name of Jesus heal this woman's finger."

Immediately, I experienced God's power and fell backwards.

Walking back to my seat I thought I could dance on cloud nine. Never before I experienced an impact of inner happiness and peace. Backing in this self satisfaction emotions shaken me. Sitting in my chair, the pastor boldly asked for confessions. I sprang to my feet, removed my finger cast, and shouted, "I'm healed. When I came tonight I had a broken finger from playing volleyball. But after hearing God's message I know I got healed."

Several people surrounding me jumped up

clapping their hands, glorifying God with 'Praise the Lord'; 'Hallelujah'; and 'Bless you God."

I know in human reality praying for a broken finger is not an in thing to do. But I realized a powerful lesson that special night. So what if I derive from an Asian American bloodline? So what if I got healed in a black congregation? As the pastor stated, "The Lord knows no racial barriers. He has no preferences."

I truly believe this can apply anytime, anywhere to anybody.

REASSURANCE AWAKENED

———————◆●◆———————

'Home' meant residing in a garage apartment. I enjoyed working split shifts cooking French fries at Rawleigh's restaurant. Terribly shy, lacking self-esteem, I acquired independence, and a stubborn attitude. Possessing hyper-charge energy I did what I wanted. After working hours, I browsed 'decent clubs.' Socializing among strangers, I displayed the latest eye-popping dance moves. God didn't exist. I asked him no favors. Life continued until February, 1981. After an exhausting day I came home. Finishing a both, I thought, "I must put on my green robe. It's going to be chilly." I relied on a box heater for extra room warmth because the radiator bathroom never seemed sufficient.

Awakening next morning, I discovered my nude body sticking to the upper sheet. Carefully prying my skin loose, I glanced at my right arm. Above the elbow rested a dark purplish, black patch. Burnt skin? Groggily, I stumbled towards the bathroom. Analyzing my body through a full-length mirror I shouted, "No!" I couldn't believe my eyes. My lower right back had burned to a crisp. My left shoulder sported an ugly burn.

I obtained a shiny left black eye, and two busted, swollen lips.

Ironically, I wasn't clothed. If clothed, I might have caught on fire, and possibly burnt to death.

I had injured myself. Being epileptic I could,

without warning have a 'fit'. Grand-mal seizures made me jerk. Having convulsions, I lost total awareness.

I noticed dried blood stains glaring from a glistening bathtub, and a porcelain basin. I noticed cooked flesh on the radiator's left front frame. Seeing this, I broke down. I cried.

Regaining composure, I reviewed the injuries. Strange, I felt nothing. Taping two gauze pads on on my arm burn, I went to work.

Andy, our 'bus boy' passed me, accidentally knocking off both pads. My boss Rawleigh asked, "What happened?" Explaining my plight, and showing him my back burn he shook his head, stating, "Jap, go to the doctor. Take the day off."

As a walk-in victim carrying no medical insurance I demanded treatment as an outpatient.

Explaining I must be treated for severe burns, I replied, "No." I received physical therapy treatment. Next day I ran a fever and cold chills. Unknown to me my body was dehydrated, prone to inner infections.

Biting pride, I staggered through Rawleigh's informing Linda, my manager, "I'm sick. I'm going to the hospital."

My doctor admitted me in a local hospital as an emergency case victim on February 5, 1981. Yes, a birthday surprise becoming a horrible nightmare. Flat on my back I had no say what to do with my life.

Three patches needed to changed. I had two physical therapy treatments a day. I dreaded them. The gauze wrapping and pads lost moisture, sticking to my burns. Imagine changing into fresh wrappings after a burn continues gluing to the old padding. Worse, I endured 'scraping' off dead skin with an instrument after soaking in a metal whirlpool tub at controlled hot temperatures. Vividly, I pictured myself gritting my teeth, and biting my tongue to hold back anguished tears.

Nurses regularly made rounds three to four hours. A light sleeper I tuned in from sheer boredom to watch television. Channel 39 won first place.

Readily, I adapted to favorite teen reruns, and to Pat Robertson's 700 Club.

I admired his faith in God. To me he had it altogether, living his life for God.

Close friends brought religious literature. Being a passionate reader I absorbed words from the Bible as a sponge absorbs water.

My physician condition worsened. My body could not produce skin. I was anemic. Talk about scenery. I was a sight displaying three patches, an I-v tube, and a hemoglobin bag, needed to rebuild red blood cells. After three weeks a surgeon stated he must perform two skin grafts. Concerned about this ordeal, I shot point blank questions.

"How long will I be on the table?"

"Anywhere from three to five hours."

"Is there a possibility I might die?"

He smiled. "Yes, but I think you've regained your strength and are young enough to make it through this operation."

Alone again in my room I felt uneasy. Weeping tears, desperately I prayed. "Forgive me. If you think my number is up I hope by your mercy I'll make it to the lowest level in Heaven."

Checking my vital signs after the operation my doctor appeared worried. Questioning the nurses he found something combined with the oxygen in my bloodstream lowering my blood pressure. A nurse stayed on duty late that evening. Each time I closed my eyes she nudged me. Later I learned if I had gone to sleep I might have died.

On his last visit the doctor replied, "You must not eat now, but only drink some 7-up. I think you can get some rest now."

I slept, feeling reassured everything was alright. Seriously.

YIELD TO GOD

Could God love me? Difficult financial burdens had blinded my spiritual insight. Bitterly, I began questioning his sincerity by reliving my past asking "Why?" Surprisingly, God revealed much needed answers at a local church meeting.

"Tonight is your night. The Lord spoke through Harper's Holy Spirit to witness you about finances.

Forget the past. You have planted a new seed, and am a new creature. You have a new beginning.

Forgive yourself. You are not guilty, and others who hurt you are not guilty. God forgives them as he forgives you. Only forgive yourself.

Tithe--with what little money you possess. Give that ten percent to the Lord.

Give up your stubbornness. Humble yourself. God is first in your life. Consult him in all matters.

Commune with God. Pray to him about other people's needs. Read the word of God (the Bible) daily.

Let go of your selfishness. It only hinders the Holy Spirit to work through you.

I emphasis let go, and trust the Lord entirely. Lean not unto through your own understanding.

The Lord gave you wisdom and strength to fight your life's hardships. However, the seed has been planted for you to release your shell of protection. Allow God to manifest the Holy Spirit to work in your life. It cannot work if you dot humble yourself in your life.

I repeat "'Give up. Give up that shell of 'I don't give a damn attitude'. Give up your prideful nature, and stubbornness.. Yield to God completely. Again, I say, 'Yield to God completely.'"

NO DOUBT

Our heavenly Father is so merciful. Who else but God can change sinner's outlook in life?

For living a loveless existence, feeling unwanted is sheer agony. Each day remains a challenge, struggling to survive countless, glum, lonely hours. Security within relies feeding upon negative attitudes.

Why? Because inner dependence stems from feeling blue, and possessing, "I don't give a damn" attitude. You conclude the majority of human race doesn't care about a neglected, abused individual.

Your bottled bitterness, and resentment are choice weapons to a target. Its ambition and goals are to build a powerful barrier, proving to society God does not exist.

Yes pride, and lies deceived me spiritually. Unexplained circumstances revealed an awareness the Holy Comforter actually existed. Experiencing a glowing feeling, I sensed Heaven's door opened. A springtime breath of mountain air sweetened the sky. Nature appeared lovely. The peaceful, self-satisfaction flowed freely to reach depths of a hungry, thirsty soul.

I'm only a new born child of God. As a babe, I cry for knowledge, and wisdom of God's truth. Eventually, through Jesus Christ, my 'mustard' seed faith continues to grow firmer, sturdier, more solid as the BOOK OF AGES.

However, I pray, "God give me strength to fight life battles. Yes, renew a weakling's courage to smile after facing defeat. Toss needed patience to endure unforeseen hardships."

Sitting upright in a burnt-orange chair, I feel happy. I'm content, anticipating no sorrow or pain. I know my invincible fortress shan't hold up forever. Unexpected turmoil may strike a hard blow. Sadly, a cornerstone weakens, and tumbling mortar fall.

Heavenly Father, you feel my pain. We unite, and fight. Fallen maybe, but not beaten. Together, we overcome obstacles, defeating Satan to receive victory.

Welcoming spiritual success, we reign victorious winners.

Thank you Lord for keeping me alive in your earthly kingdom. Use me to glorify your name in word or deed.

HONESTLY

I'm a Christian. Without a doubt, I don't question Christ's purpose on Earth or the fact that God is His Father. Seriously. Let me explain. Being unemployed, I sought work. I entered a building--I recall its background music. Listening to it penetrated my spine with chills. I shivered. Glancing behind me, I imagined Mae West flaunting husky vocal chords, telling unknown admirers, "As a woman of the world,

I can't help myself." Ahead, a platinum blonde beauty gracefully slung herself on a polished stage floor. Half perching her slender torso on her elbows, clasping petite hands together under her chin, she smiled a heavenly smile.

Politely, I clapped. Noticing her shimmering attire, I ponder, *What is this angel doing here?* Jumping up to curtsy, she smiled again, leaving quickly.

Almost desolate surroundings cried, lonely for companionship. No other person sat in the restaurant lounge except the owner. Obvious age had marred her youthful loveliness. However, underneath facial wrinkles, a pair of vivid green gemstones twinkled brightly. As she spoke with authority, I listened. "Let me finish this burger. I'm hungry,"

Patiently waiting, I thought, *What kind of job interview is this? How am I going to make money here?*

Two perspectives walked in.

"Delicious," the owner replied, daintily removing unwanted crumbs with hand-designed floral linen napkin. "Allow me to explain circumstances. Shady happenings have ruined this restaurant's reputation. We need to boost our business, providing desirable menu items and decent entertainment for an elderly audience--mainly men. Each of you must perform a song and dance ritual. I want your name, address, a telephone number where you can be reached, and your favorite type of music. Age doesn't matter."

I looked around. Tattered fringe hung limply from the upstairs balcony. Spotless starched linen tablecloths graced sturdy wooden round tables. Small vases of fresh roses adorned the middle. Velvet cushioned chairs highlighted the atmosphere. Apparently a beauty in another dimension, I outlined an elderly man admiring a dancer's movements. How?

"May I have your name?'

"Kathy."

"Such a plain name. Your stage name could be Katrina if I hired you. What taste of music do you prefer?"

"I like old rock and roll. Some blues and soul."

"Let me hear you sing."

I sang "Proud Mary," swaying to the upbeat tempo.

"Not quite what I had in mind. Could you sing a suggestive song? One a bit slower, emphasizing your movements towards the customer?'

But I couldn't. I would not make suggestive movements to an unknown stranger, gesturing about and flaunting myself to someone I didn't know. How could I sound sugar and spice in a smelly dance hall?

I realized the restaurant was a parlour; a screen to drag innocent people to desire creatures they could not obtain; a dud to fulfill a craving one desperately wanted.

"Kathy, I'm waiting."

A biblical scripture crossed me. "The spirit is willing, but the flesh is weak." I needed to work. I needed money to pay bills. Asking the band to perform "Strangers in the Night," I acted out a desperate scene. Silently, I twirled around, pointing my forefinger to a man's face. Echoes of how we met merged as one. I gave the imaginary character a "come on" sign. I yearned for approval. His eyes sparkled. I stroked his sagging arm. He smiled. The closing lines came to a halt. I pawed his weather-beaten cheeks and, stepping back, blew him a Marilyn Monroe kiss. Nodding, he gave me a thumbs-up.

Reality awoke me. I heard, "Nicely done. Be here at 7:30 tomorrow night, Katrina. By the way, my name is Miss Honeybee. I do believe you ave great potential."

I have been dancing three years. My faith in God hasn't changed. Honestly. However, face the facts. I'm not ugly. I have a curvy figure, and I can dance. America's economy is downhill. During a national recession, a woman grabs any job available. But people often raised their eyebrows after inquiring of a young minister what I do for a living. My half-brother explains that I dance in a nightclub, stating, "Well, she has to."

GOOD SAMARITAN

———•◦•———

Frustrated, I slammed the cottage screen. Bending over, staring downward, I retied a loose shoestring. I shivered. Crisp autumn breezes penetrated my thin cotton jacket. Ahead, swaying rhythmically, forest leaves seized my nostrils' attention. Anointing the atmosphere with perfume, a musky aroma lingered.

"Yikes, an awesome miracle," I muttered,

questioning my sanity. "Why in Earth's creation did I retreat here? Am I crazy or stupid?"

Inner conscience rebelled, screaming, *"Neither."*

Beckoning me, dusk whispered, *"Take your stroll, girl. Don't harbour boredom. Release your anguish."*

A flower child living freely in the Ozark Mountains, I often walked a nearby country road before sunset. Treading on worn sneakers, I acknowledged every winding turn and steepest hills. Time passed. Deeply immersed in thoughts, I realized a sky darkened, capturing itself evening shadows. "How strange," I mused. "I don't need a flashlight." Radiantly, the brightest stars and a silver full moon illuminated visible details of lonesome asphalt.

Suddenly, terror struck. A wild, savage animal swiftly raced towards me. Terrified, I could not move. Paralyzed by fear, I felt helpless. Hard core reality sank in. *My God, I'm his target--and prey.* Feelings of doom arose. Raising up hands for protection to shield my body appeared useless.

Sky, open your sweet silence. Did not rustling trees hear a woman's chilling, bloodcurdling screams? Why? An assault is happening. Earth's ground remembers. A mad dog leaps, furiously attacking an innocent victim.

Impact. A cracking sound echoed through a severe blow. Gushing blood splattered, covering my face. I could not see. Blood continued to flow.

Shaken seriously, I reminded myself, "Girl, you're conscious. You're okay, You aren't dead. You're okay."

Repeating this, I gained composure. Unbuttoning my jacket, I folded the garment in four squares. Gently, I wiped excess blood from the right facial features. Mustering every ounce of muscle, I applied heavy pressure onto a split forehead.

I walked, forcing myself to remain alert. Each dragged step seemed precious, representing a priceless pieced of eternity.

Dim lights appeared. A miracle? Unknowingly, I had reached an emergency care unit. I knocked.

"Sorry, we are closed."

I pounded harder, screaming, "Please help me! Please!"

Releasing the door's lock, a young man appeared. Gasping, he shouted, "Oh my goodness!. Come in; come in!"

He ushered me to a bed. Immediately after he cleaned my wound with hydrogen peroxide, I asked, "Do I need stitches?"

"Oh yes, quite a few."

"Well, can you stitch me up?"

"Yes, I think so."

Numbing my forehead with anesthetic, he slowly began sewing. Fully conscious, I thought, *This dude is forever taking his time. Will he ever finish?* Patiently, I waited counting each completed stitch.

Twelve stitches completed, I heard, "Um, not a bad job. I think this will do. Need a way home?"

"Yes."

Totally exhausted, I don't remember much about

the trip. Did he say, "I'm not authorized to perform an operation. Please don't mention this?"

Vaguely, I recall stating, "Really? Yeah, I guess so."

Weeks passed. Curiosity overwhelmed me. I asked the care unit his name.

A perky receptionist answered, "Oh, you must mean Don. An odd person, but very nice. He no longer works here, but he was the night cleanup person for the building. These youngsters nowadays don't hold down a job. Always roaming the countryside."

Smiling, nodding my head, I replied, "I suppose. Well, thank you. You have a nice day."

"You too."

I walked away, thinking, *Ah, so Don is the hero. Thanks buddy--wherever you are.*

NOT FOR ME

I had a good childhood. Mama and Daddy argued, but never to the point they physically abused each other. Mom scolded us kids,(my older brother and two younger sisters); and my father disciplined us by given whippings. Believe me, being a rowdy kid, I saw my share of "The Belt.'

I must have been four or five old when Grandpa let me taste beer from a sip of his bottle. The liquid was bitter, but pleasant. Mama jumped on Grandpa's case. I asked myself, 'Why?' My parents were social drinkers. I saw them drink alcohol at parties, family reunions, and during holidays. In fact, all my parents' friends, and my aunts and uncles drank ed.

Well, by the time I was eight years old I didn't see anything wrong with me drinking a beer or two. I remember sneaking me a drink occasionally at Granny's house. She had a backyard in ground swimming pool. Us kids 'played', and watched the grownups 'get happy.'

So alcohol was around me quite a bit.

I hated school. I rebelled by drinking. Beer wasn't hard to get. Being a good-size kid, I looked old enough to buy beer. And in my freshman year I really got going with my drinking. I worked through school. I had my own car. I kept an ice chest supplied full of cold beer. My school had open campus, and oh so easy to get a drink or two or three.

I enjoyed the camping trips Daddy took on

weekends. By now he couldn't do anything about my drinking. However, I guess he figured since I worked, bought my own booze, he gave up trying to stop me.

I never felt happy. I didn't understand why I felt depressed . To me drinking was a way out of depression. I reasoned if I left home, left my so-called drinking buddies behind, and started with a clean slate, my life would become better. I tried. I found a good paying job; lost it; and had to go job hunting to pay rent for a three bedroom home. Wham! Some idiot rear end my Oldsmobile. Put me in the hospital, and out of work. After staying a long spell in a four cornered room I started drinking hard liquor. I put away a fifth of whiskey or tequila, and also beer a day.

I believed in working. I kept my drinking away from work. I might not enjoy a job, but I do enjoy getting paid. Without money I couldn't get loaded. That was top propriety in my life.

Anyway, I lost several 'loves of my life' because each time I partied, I got plastered, and showed the world my true nature. One instance, drunk as a skunk, I broke up with someone. I went to jail three occasions over our broken relationship.

I love my freedom, and was getting to the point being 'sick and tired' of ' being sick of tired'. I'm tired not knowing my own direction. I re dedicated my life to God, and figured with his help I can make it . I didn't want to get by living from paycheck to paycheck. I wanted something more in life than waking up in a stranger's bed not remembering what happened the night before. I didn't want any more DWI, public intoxication fines or domestic violence fines. I couldn't escape being in jail. I know drinking got me in this mess. But I know what I had to do once I got out. Sure, I have to clean up my act completely. It will be hard; but it can be done.

I want to succeed. I figured the money I wasted on alcohol, clubbing, chasing the opposite sex, and bailing myself out of jail could be used in getting a nice car. In a few years maybe I could have a home and some land.

So all in all, alcohol is not for me. I cannot handle it. It handles me. That is not the way it supposed to be. So I will take the help available to me to quit drinking for good. I will start living THE GOOD LIFE.

REVELATION

Thirty years ago, a cherished girlfriend taught me a valuable lesson. After confiding intimate secrets her eyes darted. Pleading, she whined, "Remember this between you and me. Don't speak to it to anybody."

I felt smug. Our bond existed in a no broken truce.

I betrayed her. I broke my vow. Feeling guilty, I

apologized. Listened, nodding he head she hugged my neck saying, "Don't think anything of it. We've only human."

Why did this woman love me, despite the fact I treated her wrongly?

She possessed compassion. I discovered 'opening' doors, portrayed chapters in a lifetime. 'Sections' are seams of life unraveled to reveal hidden emotions or actions.

After the incident I concluded, "Whether we realize it or not, our parents behavior toward us in childhood centers us in a spot light. They connect us to an outer world. Even though we strive to be somebody in our fleshly bodies, we try to please earthly expectations, acting out regulations society wants us to follow.

An opened door can shape buried thoughts or attitudes we possess. What our spiritual lives could be had we opened another section? How different our lives could be had we taken another route? Our personal self satisfaction could be overflowing inside. Cultivated as individual seeds, our compassion towards other people could strive, spouting to become a beautiful flower."

Remember the rose? A closed door conceal buried thorns. Pushing through obstacles, but nourished with kindness and love, a determined plant bloom Hidden petals flourish in displaying magnificent petals.